For my youngest nieces, April Lyon and Catherine Durant A.D.
For my three, not so little, tigers! D.B.

This edition produced for The Book People Ltd.,
Hall Wood Avenue, Haydock, St. Helens, WA11 9UL

First published in hardback in Great Britain by HarperCollins Children's Books in 2004
First published in paperback in 2005
1 3 5 7 9 10 8 6 4 2

ISBN: 0-00-776990-3

Text copyright © Alan Durant 2004
Illustrations copyright © Debbie Boon 2004

HarperCollins Children's Books is a division of HarperCollins Publishers Ltd.

The author and illustrator assert the moral right to be identified as the author and illustrator of the work.
A CIP catalogue record for this title is available from the British Library.

Visit our website at: www.harpercollinschildrensbooks.co.uk

Printed and bound in Thailand

If You Go Walking in Tiger Wood

by Alan Durant · illustrated by Debbie Boon

HarperCollins *Children's Books*

If you go walking in Tiger Wood,

you'd better be good.

The tigers might be watching...

Look up there,
in that tree!
Is that a
TIGER?

No, it's Gibbon.

"Hello, Gibbon!"

"Boo!"

says Gibbon.

If you go skipping in Tiger Wood,
you'd better watch out,
you'd better not SHOUT!
The tigers might be listening...

Look there,

behind that bush!

Is THAT a tiger?

No, it's Deer.

"Hello, Deer!"

"Can I come too?"
says Deer.

If you go dancing in Tiger Wood,
you'd better not scream,
or splash in the stream.
The tigers might be resting…

Look there,
in that hole!
Is that a
TIGER?

No, it's Porcupine.

"Hello, Porcupine!"

"Hey, what's happening?"
says Porcupine.

If you go playing in Tiger Wood,
don't pick the leaves, don't kick the trees.
The tigers might be prowling...

Look there,
in the grass!
Could THAT be a tiger?

No, it's Peacock.
"Hello, Peacock!"

"Wait for me!"
says Peacock.

If you go walking in Tiger Wood,
you'd better be good.
The tigers might be hiding...

But where can they be?

Shall we take a look and see?

SHALL WE?

DARE WE?

But, "Stop,
don't run away!"
the tigers say.

"We've been watching you in Tiger Wood
and we know you've been good.
Please stay and play."

And we cry,
"Hooray!"

And we stayed and we played
for the rest of the day!